Dear Parent:

Congratulations! Your child is taking the first steps on an exciting journey. The destination? Independent reading!

STEP INTO READING® will help your child get there. The program offers books at five levels that accompany children from their first attempts at reading to reading success. Each step includes fun stories, fiction and nonfiction, and colorful art. There are also Step into Reading Sticker Books, Step into Reading Math Readers, and Step into Reading Phonics Readers— a complete literacy program with something to interest every child.

Learning to Read, Step by Step!

Ready to Read Preschool–Kindergarten
• big type and easy words • rhyme and rhythm • picture clues
For children who know the alphabet and are eager to begin reading.

Reading with Help Preschool–Grade 1
• basic vocabulary • short sentences • simple stories
For children who recognize familiar words and sound out new words with help.

Reading on Your Own Grades 1–3
• engaging characters • easy-to-follow plots • popular topics
For children who are ready to read on their own.

Reading Paragraphs Grades 2–3
• challenging vocabulary • short paragraphs • exciting stories
For newly independent readers who read simple sentences with confidence.

Ready for Chapters Grades 2–4
• chapters • longer paragraphs • full-color art
For children who want to take the plunge into chapter books but still like colorful pictures.

STEP INTO READING® is designed to give every child a successful reading experience. The grade levels are only guides. Children can progress through the steps at their own speed, developing confidence in their reading, no matter what their grade.

Remember, a lifetime love of reading starts with a single step!

To Will, who makes every day fun.
—A.P.S.

www.stepintoreading.com

Educators and librarians, for a variety of teaching tools, visit us at
www.randomhouse.com/teachers

Library of Congress Cataloging-in-Publication Data
Posner-Sanchez, Andrea.
Bambi's hide-and-seek / by Andrea Posner-Sanchez ; illustrated by Isidre Monés.
    p.   cm. — (Step into reading. A step 1 book)
SUMMARY: As Bambi and Thumper play hide and seek, Bambi discovers animal friends
behind bushes, in holes, up trees, and among the flowers.
ISBN 0-7364-1347-2 (trade) — ISBN 0-7364-8009-9 (lib. bdg.)
[1. Deer—Fiction.   2. Rabbits—Fiction.   3. Animals—Fiction.   4. Hide-and-seek—Fiction.]
I. Monés, Isidre, ill.   II. Title.   PZ7.P83843   Bam   2003   [E]—dc21   2002151941

Printed in the United States of America   11 10 9 8 7 6 5 4 3

STEP INTO READING, RANDOM HOUSE, and the Random House colophon are registered
trademarks of Random House, Inc.

WALT DISNEY's Bambi

Bambi's
Hide-and-Seek

by Andrea Posner-Sanchez
illustrated by Isidre Monés

Random House 🏠 New York

Bambi.

Thumper.

Hide-and-seek!

Counting.

Hiding.

Is that Thumper behind the bush?

That is not Thumper!

"Shh!"

Inside the tree?

Nuts!

That is not Thumper!

In the creek?

That is not Thumper!

"Ribbit!"

By the log?

Tap, tap, tap.

"You are not Thumper!"
says Bambi.

Bambi rests.

"Achoo!"

There is Thumper!

"Let's play again!"